THE DARK KNIGHT

CAT COMMANDER

WRITTEN BY
J.E. BRIGHT

ILLUSTRATED BY
LUCIANO VECCHIO

BATMAN CREATED BY BOB KANE
WITH BILL FINGER

RAINTREE IS AN IMPRINT OF CAPSTONE GLOBAL LIBRARY LIMITED,
A COMPANY INCORPORATED IN ENGLAND AND WALES HAVING ITS
REGISTERED OFFICE AT 264 BANBURY ROAD, OXFORD, OX2 7DY -
REGISTERED COMPANY NUMBER: 6695582

WWW.RAINTREE.CO.UK
MYORDERS@RAINTREE.CO.UK

APPLICATIONS FOR THE COPYRIGHT OWNER'S WRITTEN
PERMISSION SHOULD BE ADDRESSED TO THE PUBLISHER.

ART DIRECTOR: BOB LENTZ
DESIGNER: BRANN GARVEY

ISBN 978 1 4747 3293 2
20 19 18 17 16
10 9 8 7 6 5 4 3 2 1

BRITISH LIBRARY CATALOGUING IN PUBLICATION DATA
A FULL CATALOGUE RECORD FOR THIS BOOK IS AVAILABLE
FROM THE BRITISH LIBRARY.

Printed and bound in China

CONTENTS

WHILE STILL A BOY, BRUCE WAYNE WITNESSED THE BRUTAL MURDER OF HIS PARENTS. THE TRAGIC EVENT CHANGED THE YOUNG BILLIONAIRE FOREVER. BRUCE VOWED TO RID GOTHAM CITY OF EVIL AND KEEP ITS PEOPLE SAFE FROM CRIME. AFTER YEARS OF TRAINING HIS BODY AND MIND, HE DONNED A NEW UNIFORM AND A NEW IDENTITY.

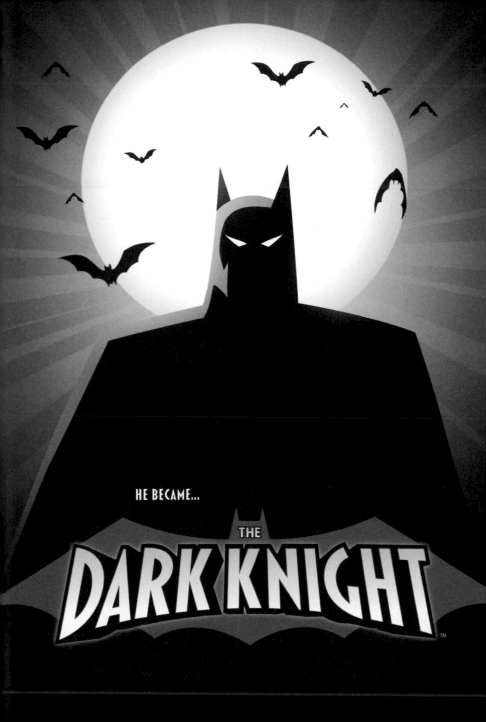

CHAPTER 1

HIGH SECURITY

On the roof of Gotham Museum, Batman stood motionless in the moonlit shadow of an air conditioning unit.

Downstairs, the party celebrating the museum's newest exhibition was starting. Batman could hear the limousines approaching. He could hear crowds cheering and reporters squawking about the arrival of celebrities.

He had been invited, of course – as his alter ego, billionaire Bruce Wayne.

In fact, Bruce was one of the biggest patrons of this exhibition of rare Ancient Egyptian artefacts, most of which had never been shown in the United States. He would join the party soon.

But first, he was going to patrol the roof – as Batman. Security couldn't be strong enough when the museum was full of such ancient treasures. Any one of the rare artefacts downstairs would fetch a fortune on the black market.

Gotham's burglars wouldn't be able to resist trying to steal something. The valuable artefacts were as tempting to them as catnip is to a cat. And now was the time for them to strike – before the galleries were open. The museum guards were busy protecting the arriving elite as they entered the reception hall.

Batman shifted deeper into the shadows. He watched beams of light dance against the cloudy night sky that were shining up from near the museum's entrance. He listened intently, on high alert.

TAP! TAP! TAP!

A scuffling noise came from across the roof. *Burglars*, Batman knew.

Batman smiled. He had trained himself to think like a criminal, and he was always pleased when his training paid off. It was so important to be able to guess what thieves would do before they even knew what their own plans were.

Keeping his body completely still, Batman swivelled his head and zeroed in on the source of the sound. He caught sight of a man in a black ski mask.

The burglar was hoisting himself over the edge of the roof railing. Batman watched silently as the muscular man leaned over the railing and helped two more masked men climb up.

The men quickly scanned the area, but they didn't see Batman in the dark shadows. Then they whispered to each other and headed towards the main elevator shaft in the middle of the roof.

As the burglars crept closer to his hidden location, the Dark Knight got ready to pounce.

"We've got to hurry," said the leader. "The show has started. We have fifteen minutes before they move from the reception hall into the galleries. So now's the time for our party."

"No," Batman spoke from the shadows. "This is *my* party."

The three robbers froze at the sound of Batman's voice. The Dark Knight was already jumping at them.

FLAP! FLAP! FLAP!

His cape billowed behind him as he landed in the middle of the burglars. Immediately, the hero flattened one crook with a kick to his knee. The robber howled and fell to the ground.

"I'm out of here!" the skinniest robber cried. He turned to flee, but Batman caught his ankle with his boot and tripped him. He hit the ground with a **THUDDDDDDDD!**

Only the muscular leader was left standing. The masked criminal pulled out a wicked-looking club.

"Bring it, Batman," the crook said with a sneer. "You're not so tough."

"You don't think so?" Batman asked. "Try me."

With a yell, the masked burglar lunged at Batman with the weapon. But Batman simply sidestepped his attack, swirling his cape like a bullfighter. As the robber stumbled past him, the Dark Knight whacked him on the back of the head with the side of his fist. *CLUNKKKKKKK!*

The muscular burglar sprawled onto the roof and let go of the club. The weapon skittered across the floor.

Before the leader could get up, Batman grabbed him by the back of his jacket. He threw the robber into the side of the air conditioner, knocking him out cold.

The Dark Knight tied up the three robbers and left them bound to a TV satellite dish. He called Commissioner Gordon and let him know to send police to the roof to pick them up.

Then the super hero hurried down to the alley behind the museum to meet Alfred in one of his limousines.

"All clear on the roof, Master Bruce?" asked his loyal butler.

"It is now," Batman replied.

With the top of the museum secured, Batman felt confident that the priceless treasures inside were safe for the night. He had helped Commissioner Gordon choose the guards at all the museum's entrances, and he had personally inspected the building's security cameras and alarms.

Nobody was going to steal any of the Ancient Egyptian artefacts on his watch.

In the time it took Alfred to drive around to the front of the museum, Batman changed into a sharp tuxedo. He stepped out of the limo as the last guests were entering the front doors.

Bruce climbed the museum stairs. He was pleased when the guards stopped him and asked for his identification and invitation. Even though they recognized him, it meant that they were taking their security jobs seriously. He was also happy to discover that Alfred had thoughtfully put the invitation in the inside tuxedo pocket.

After passing the guards, Bruce walked into the museum. He headed down the corridor towards the reception area, nodding at socialites along the way.

The reception room was a big, fancy chamber with long, white curtains framing the windows and silver chandeliers dangling overhead. A few of the museum's less-famous paintings hung on the walls, flanked by marble statues. In the main area of the room, tall, round tables covered by white tablecloths had been set up. Celebrities gathered around them, eating appetizers and drinking champagne.

Bruce smiled as Warren Pickering, the museum's director, met him near the room's entrance. "Bruce!" Mr Pickering said, "so great to see you. Thanks to your generosity, the Egyptian Antiquities exhibition is simply stunning."

"I can't wait to see it," Bruce replied. "I'm sure your museum has displayed the artefacts to their best advantage."

Mr Pickering nodded. "We'll be opening the galleries in a few moments," he said. "Now please enjoy our little party."

Bruce shook Mr Pickering's hand. Then he made his way towards a waiter carrying a tray of appetizers. His exercise on the roof had made him hungry.

The waiter handed Bruce a napkin. Bruce took a small cracker from the tray. The cracker was topped with a strange-looking pinkish mush. Bruce sniffed it and wrinkled his nose. It smelled . . . unpleasant.

"Maybe it tastes better than it looks," Bruce said.

The waiter simply nodded, so Bruce popped the cracker into his mouth. It was disgusting.

Bruce quickly spat the chewed-up cracker into his napkin. "I think the museum needs a new caterer," Bruce told the waiter. "This tastes like cat food."

"How would you know?" asked a familiar female voice behind him. "Have you eaten cat food?"

Bruce turned around and raised an eyebrow. He was facing a beautiful woman who he knew all too well.

It was Selina Kyle.

Catwoman.

CHAPTER 2

THE JEWELLED SISTRUM

Selina smiled at Bruce. She was wearing a shimmering black dress and a fetching necklace. Bruce knew that inside her beautiful exterior beat a sly, mischievous heart. As Catwoman, she was one of the most successful thieves in the world. She was also a martial arts expert and skilled at using a whip.

Still, despite the trouble she caused, Bruce was happy to see her. The secret hero had always respected her as a fellow prowler of the night.

"Selina," Bruce said, smiling. "I hope you're on your best behaviour tonight."

"Oh, Bruce," Selina purred, putting her hand on his arm. Her fingernails were long, sharp and painted black. "I'm always on my best behaviour. We simply have different definitions of what that means."

Bruce laughed. "True," he said, putting his hand over hers. "So, are you excited to see this exhibition?"

"Absolutely," Selina replied. "I've been looking forward to it for weeks. The Ancient Egyptians and I have much in common. You've heard of my fondness for cats?"

"I think I may have heard that, yes," Bruce answered coyly.

Selina pushed a strand of long hair behind her ear.

"The Ancient Egyptians were as mad for cats as I am," she said. "They were the first to let felines into their homes, and they were even known to worship cats. One of their goddesses, Bastet, had the body of a beautiful woman and the head of a cat. She was the goddess of protection against thieves, rats and snakes . . . and she also was the goddess of dancing and music."

"I can see how you would relate," said Bruce. "Although protection against thieves might cause you some problems."

"Oh, Bruce," Selina said. "Aren't you funny."

"Excuse me!" Mr Pickering, the museum director, cried. "Ladies and gentlemen, thank you for coming tonight. I'm pleased to announce that our gallery of Ancient Egyptian artefacts is now open for viewing!"

Selina held out her arm for Bruce to take. "Shall we?" she asked.

"We shall," Bruce replied. He linked his elbow with hers and led her towards the gallery doors.

Inside the exhibition room, the lighting was amber-coloured and dim. A narrow overhead spotlight illuminated each display case so that the artefacts seemed to glow. Bruce and Selina strolled past the cases, looking at finely made silver necklaces, delicate decorated pottery, jade scarab beetles and tablets engraved with hieroglyphics.

Selina stopped in front of a podium that had an unusual object encased under a glass dome. The artefact was made of a golden hoop with a long handle. It stood upright in the case.

Across the hoop were three crossbars, on which jewelled rings hung. The handle was inlaid with luminous emeralds. Selina peered into the case, smiling.

"What is that?" Bruce asked.

"It's a sistrum," Selina explained. "It's a type of musical instrument, jangled like a rattle or a tambourine. The goddess Bastet is often depicted holding one in her hand. Sistrum means 'to shake', and the instruments usually provided rhythm for dancing or were played softly in religious ceremonies. This is the finest one ever discovered. The piece has many legends written about it. It's gorgeous, isn't it?"

"Beautiful," agreed Bruce.

Selina sighed. "I've always wanted one," she said wistfully.

"Don't get any ideas," Bruce said. "There are guards and metal detectors at every exit of this museum."

"You don't say," replied Selina with an arched eyebrow.

They continued browsing through the exhibition, peering at jackal-headed statues, marble urns and glittering amulets.

Soon, Selina led Bruce to a painting on a fragment of a tomb wall. The artwork was faded, but Bruce could see that it showed two rows of workers pulling an enormous stone block to a partially completed pyramid.

"The workers who built the pyramids weren't slaves, you know," Selina said. "They weren't prisoners, either. The more skilled ones were paid well."

"Good to know," said Bruce. "Slavery is evil. Deciding that we could own other people was one of humanity's worst mistakes."

Selina let go of Bruce's arm. "And yet we let it go on every day in Gotham City," she whispered.

Turning to face her, Bruce frowned. "What do you mean?" he asked.

"Cats," Selina replied. "Dogs, too. All animals, really. It's fine to have pets, but legally, people now own their pets. People shouldn't be allowed to own other living creatures. It's slavery, pure and simple. At most, we should only be allowed to adopt them as their guardians. Or, to use a term you'd understand, Bruce . . . as their wards."

Bruce nodded. "I've heard that argument," he said. "There are laws protecting cats and other pets from abuse, but yes, pets are legally considered property. There's a movement to have pet owners called guardians instead, but it's a long legal process."

"It's too slow," said Selina.

"Well," Bruce said with a shrug, "it's not like the cats have organized a union."

"Not yet," Selina replied. Her mobile phone beeped, and she pulled it out of her small handbag. "Oh," she said, "I'm sorry, Bruce, but I have to go."

"Everything's all right, I hope," said Bruce.

"*Purr*fectly," said Selina. "It's been lovely to see you."

Bruce kissed her cheek. "You, too," he said. "I hope we'll be seeing one another again soon."

"Undoubtedly," Selina said, and she hurried out of the exhibition hall.

Bruce resumed wandering around the gallery. He peered into the cases at the ancient treasures and greeted the other patrons. Only a few minutes after Selina left, there was a commotion in the middle of the room.

"Look!" someone said.

A small crowd gathered around one of the displays. Bruce moved closer. The jewelled sistrum flickered in its case.

"What's happening?" a woman asked.

Bruce glanced up at the spotlight on the ceiling above the sistrum's case.

Instead of pure white light, the fixture above was projecting multiple colours. He held his hand in the spotlight's beam, and the sistrum disappeared.

The crowd gasped. When Bruce pulled his hand away, the sistrum reappeared in the case, although shimmering like a poor quality movie. "It's a hologram," he said.

Warren Pickering pushed his way through the crowd to stand at Bruce's side. "Impossible," he said. "I placed the sistrum on that podium myself. The original must have been stolen!"

"If it was, it's still in the museum," Bruce said. "Nobody could have gotten past the metal detectors with it. And I know all the guards personally. Is there anyone on staff who might be suspect?" he asked the museum director.

"Nobody," Mr Pickering replied. "They're all our best people. Even the caterer for the party came with the highest recommendations . . . she knew you, in fact."

Bruce narrowed his eyes. "That's a problem," he said. "The caterer could have smuggled out the sistrum with the dirty dishes and leftovers. Who was it?"

"You were talking to her earlier," Mr Pickering answered. "Selina Kyle."

"Of course it was," said Bruce.

CHAPTER 3

BATS, CATS AND RATS

As soon as he got home to Wayne Manor, Bruce hurried down to the Batcave and began searching for information on Selina's whereabouts. His computer system was linked into all of Gotham City's databases and surveillance equipment.

He tapped into the government records, but there was no listing for Selina Kyle anywhere. She had no driving license under her name that Bruce could find. No phone. No utility services. No cable TV. No credit card history or bank accounts or bills.

Not even a library card.

Most incredible was that Selina had no police record, either. Bruce knew she had been arrested several times. As Batman, he'd put her in prison himself!

For someone who had lived in Gotham City for years, Selina had done an amazing job of covering her tracks. Somehow she'd managed to clear her name from the grid entirely. Or almost entirely.

The next day, Bruce discovered an old posting on the backlog of an online community bulletin board. A female with the screen name "SelKy" was searching for a cat-sitter for a "large number of felines". It was a small lead, but it was something.

Bruce traced SelKy's computer address to a swanky downtown condo.

Bruce waited until night fell. Then, as Batman, he drove the Batmobile downtown and parked in an alley not far from the condo. The Dark Knight scrambled up a fire escape to the rooftop of a tall building, and hopped over until he was on top of the correct condominium. With a grappling hook and wire, he rappelled down the side of the high-rise to the floor of Selina's last possible address.

CLICK CLICK CLICK! With a skinny metal tool from his Utility Belt, Batman easily jammed the window open. He slipped inside, using his torch to search the darkened condo.

It was tastefully decorated, with cream-coloured furniture against dark walls. The rooms didn't look abandoned – just empty.

There was a stand of healthy plants in

the living room in front of a big window. It was a beautiful condo, but there were no personal items or pictures anywhere. The apartment could have belonged to anyone.

In the kitchen, Batman found a note stuck to the refrigerator with a cat magnet.

Bat –

Welcome to my pad.

I took the cats.

Please be a dear and water my plants.

XOXO

– Cat

Batman smiled. Catwoman was one jump ahead of him.

After a thorough search, Batman found no more information.

The Dark Knight watered Selina's plants and then headed home.

When Batman arrived back at the Batcave, he found Alfred sitting in front of a bank of computer terminals. News reports played on a few screens, and graphs and maps illuminated other monitors.

"Ah, Master Bruce," said Alfred. "There you are. I've been following this quite interesting news story. It seems that all day a single area of Gotham has been hit by a rash of missing or runaway cats. The 31st Police Precinct has been swamped with phone calls – hundreds of them – about the lost pets."

Batman peered at the TV screen, which showed a sad lady being interviewed about her missing cat. She was holding up a picture of a fat orange tabby.

"Hundreds of cats going missing at the same time can't be a coincidence," Bruce said.

"I agree," replied Alfred. "Some of the cats simply couldn't be found, but many of the owners saw them escaping through windows and dashing out open doors, apparently in a hurry to get somewhere. I thought it was quite peculiar, so I took the liberty of plotting the reports on a map of the area."

Alfred touched the computer monitor and a grid popped up – a map of the 31st Precinct. A circular starburst pattern of red dots showed the location of the homes where missing cats had been reported. The pattern covered an eight-block radius, and was sparser at the edges. It was denser with dots towards the centre, where it became solid red.

"The centre point," said Batman, rubbing his chin. "Some of the cats escaped from their homes, as though they were being . . . summoned, correct?"

"It would be fair to make that assumption," replied Alfred.

Batman nodded. "So they were called by something near that central location."

"Also a fairly logical leap," said the loyal butler.

Turning sharply, Batman strode towards his Batcycle. "Then I should go and check out that centre point," he decided. "Send the coordinates to the cycle's GPS, Alfred."

"Yes, Master Bruce," replied Alfred. "I have already done so."

Zooming on his Batcycle, Batman blasted down the dark streets of Gotham.

The centre point location turned out to be in the middle of a residential neighbourhood of fancy townhouses and small apartments near Robinson Park.

When Batman pulled up in front of the specified spot, he found himself outside a spacious Italian restaurant with its windows covered with brown paper. According to a sign on the door, the restaurant had been shut down by the Department of Health due to rats and mice in the kitchen.

The restaurant appeared dark and quiet.

CLANK CLINK CLICK! Batman quietly slid the lock on the front door and stepped into the dim dining room.

Nobody was inside. All the furniture had been pushed to the sides of the room and neatly stacked – except for one table in the middle.

The centre table had a red tablecloth and a single, flickering candle on it. Batman cautiously approached the table. On it was another note:

Bat –

This restaurant used to have a divine chicken cacciatore.

I took the cats.

When the cats are away, the mice will play.

And the rats.

– Cat

Batman frowned, blew out the candle, and turned on his torch. That's when he heard a scratching noise from the back of the restaurant — from behind the kitchen door.

Maybe Catwoman had accidentally left one of the stolen cats behind. Batman strode to the door and opened it, shining his torch down onto the floor.

A little grey mouse blinked up at him. It squeaked, grabbed the crumb it had been nibbling, and scurried away. Batman followed it with the torch's beam.

With the circle of light, he trailed the mouse over to a large, gnawed hole in the wall, where it disappeared inside. As soon as his torch beam hit the dark hole, the space began churning with furry bodies. Tiny eyes glittered in the light.

Then a fat, mean-looking rat scurried out of the hole. It was followed by many more rats and mice, all racing towards Batman. The hole erupted with filthy rodents.

SQUEAK! SQUEAK! SQUEAK!

Wave after wave of rats were spewing out into the kitchen!

There wasn't much that Batman feared. He had spent his adulthood instilling terror in the criminals of Gotham. He was a super hero who had battled vile evil-doers since he'd first put on his mask and cape.

Batman had no desire to fight a thousand angry rats in a cramped kitchen. They swarmed around him, biting his boots.

GNAW! GNAW! GNAW!

Even with Batman jumping around, the rats climbed up on top of each other to claw their way up his legs.

Batman turned, leaped over the sea of

rodents, and ran.

The rats and mice chased him through the dining room and out into the street.

Batman jumped onto the Batcycle and tore away into the night.

The last thing he saw in his rear view mirror was thousands of rats pouring onto the streets of Precinct 31.

CHAPTER 4

THE ULTIMATUM

Batman drove the Batcycle directly to Gotham Central, the police headquarters. On the way, he messaged Commissioner James Gordon to meet him on the roof.

"It's been a quiet night, mostly," said Commissioner Gordon when Batman arrived near the Bat-Signal projector. "But you never show up with good news."

Batman's lips twitched. "Tonight's no different," he said. "Unsurprisingly, Catwoman is behind all of the cat disappearances."

"What concerns me is how fast the rodent population moved into the area as soon as the cats were gone," Batman said. "In less than a day, their numbers were . . . impressive."

"Are you telling me that the house cats are what keep the rats in check?" Commissioner Gordon asked. "I thought it was the millions of dollars we spend in rodent control every year."

"It's a balance," replied Batman. "There are too many rodents to wipe out completely with poison. Apparently, the cats have acted as a deterrent – their presence has helped to keep the mice and rats underground. With the balance upset, the rats feel bold enough to swarm."

Commissioner Gordon sighed.

"Extremely bad health issues arise when the rat population grows out of control," Gordon said. "They spread diseases. They can make whole neighbourhoods uninhabitable. And they could ruin our food and water supply."

"Catwoman has proven she can control the cats, at least in a limited area," said Batman. "And if she controls the cats, she controls the rats . . . and all of Gotham."

"What does she want?" Commissioner Gordon asked.

"I'm not entirely certain," said Batman. "But I'll bet we find out soon. Tomorrow afternoon, most people in the city will be watching the Gotham Wildcats play in the Deco Bowl. I assume she'll take advantage of the game to reach the whole city at once."

Commissioner Gordon nodded. "I'll boost security at the game."

"And I'll do what I can to find Catwoman," said Batman. "And stop her."

*   *   *

Back in the Batcave, Batman worked through the night preparing his computer equipment to build an electronic net to catch Catwoman. He hacked into the television network systems and rigged triggers to trace her signal if she tried to hijack the Deco Bowl broadcast. Batman also programmed his city-wide surveillance systems to automatically report anything else out of the ordinary.

Early in the morning, Alfred entered the Batcave carrying a young cat.

"Cute," said Batman. "Our new pet?"

Alfred stroked the cat. "Maybe," he said. "Or perhaps we could use her as our little spy. If Catwoman summons the cats, there's no reason why Gladys here wouldn't be culled. We could trace her with a microchip in her collar."

"Excellent idea, Alfred," said Batman.

"Yes, sir," Alfred said. He put Gladys down on the floor of the Batcave. He and Batman watched as she slunk about the hideout, exploring. After sniffing around, Gladys hopped up onto an empty cushioned desk chair, curled up and purred.

"She feels right at home," said Alfred with a sly grin. "I will leave you two to get better acquainted, I think. I shall return shortly with some breakfast – for both of you."

Before Alfred could go upstairs, Gladys perked up, her eyes wide and ears raised.

Just then, Batman saw a cluster of small brown bats flutter into the Batcave, returning from their night out. Gladys watched them intently as they roosted together, hanging upside down in a huddle on the cave's ceiling.

"I don't care how useful you are," Batman said to the cat. "If you catch a single bat, you're out of here."

*   *   *

The Deco Bowl started at midday. Batman watched the game on two monitors. One showed the network coverage, and the other showed an all-sports channel. He also kept a close eye on his computer systems analyzing the source and strength of the networks' signal.

Bruce had secretly rerouted the signal to bounce through his own personal satellite before it was broadcast. That way, he could pinpoint the location of the sources, which were currently coming from the networks' headquarters.

Batman had rooted for the Wildcats his whole life. Wayne Enterprises was a major donor to the popular annual charity event against the Metropolis Meteors. This year, the teams seemed evenly matched. The Meteors had a strong passing game, but the Wildcats' defensive line was great. They were tied 7–7 at half-time.

By the middle of the fourth quarter, Batman was so involved in the game that he had almost forgotten about Catwoman. Despite the Wildcats' efforts, the Meteors had managed to score another touchdown.

However, their extra point was blocked, making the score 7–13. Now the Wildcats were in control again, and had been steadily forcing the ball towards the Meteors' end zone all quarter.

With the clock running out on the final fourth down, the Wildcat quarterback snapped the ball to one of the team's best runners. With three Meteors hot on his heels, the runner raced towards the end zone.

Batman stood up. The runner was only ten yards away, dodging a Meteors player swooping in from the side. Then five yards from tying the score –

KIRSSSSSSSSSSSSSHHH!

The network picture flickered on the screen.

The football game was replaced by an image of Catwoman lying sideways on a golden sofa. She was dressed in a white, Egyptian gown and wearing a silver crown below the ears of her cat mask. In one hand, she held the jewelled sistrum. She was surrounded by relaxed cats. "Greetings, Gotham City," she purred.

Batman imagined he could hear the angry cry of surprised football fans echo for miles around. Although disappointed at missing the game's outcome, he sprang into action, trying to pinpoint the location of her signal.

"My apologies for interrupting the coverage of your little game," Catwoman continued, "but what I have to tell you today is more important." She paused to scratch the head of a long-haired cat.

"For too long," she said, "my furry feline friends have not been given the respect and equality they deserve. As the law stands now, humans own cats as property, and that is simple slavery. We can be their keepers, or their guardians, or their friends, but the law must be changed so that humans are no longer the *owners* of cats. I am hereby requesting that a new law be written that makes it clear that cats are not our property."

Catwoman sat up on the sofa. She gave the sistrum a quick shake. All the cats around her snapped to attention, shifting closer. "This law must be passed by midnight tonight . . . or the choice will be taken out of your hands."

Batman's software had almost pinned down her location.

In a few seconds, Batman would have her exact address.

"I will take all your cats," said Catwoman sternly. "You will no longer deserve their company. And then, as you can already tell, Gotham City will belong to the rats."

Catwoman smiled, and the camera slowly zoomed in on her lips until her grin filled the whole screen. "But if you ask me," she said with a sly hiss, "Gotham's already run by rats – and fat cats, if you'll pardon the expression."

KIRSSSSSSSSSSSSSSSH!

The image flickered and flashed back to the football field. The Gotham Wildcats were dancing happily in the Meteors' end zone.

Batman checked his computer again.

His satellite had narrowed in on a location. An animation of a globe popped up on the screen, spinning as it focused.

Then, finally, the globe stopped revolving.

Batman groaned.

Catwoman must have realized Batman would try to trace her broadcast position. She had routed the signal through international channels to give a false report of her whereabouts.

The Dark Knight's monitor showed a flashing light on the globe. It displayed Catwoman's current location as a city in Tibet – way up high in the Himalayan Mountains.

Kathmandu.

Batman couldn't help but grin at Catwoman's twisted sense of humour.

"Funny," Batman growled. "But not really."

CHAPTER 5

MADDER THAN A WET CAT

It didn't matter whether or not Batman thought Catwoman had a point that cats shouldn't be owned. Once she tried to blackmail Gotham City, she had to be brought to justice.

The problem was finding her. She was certainly in Gotham, not Kathmandu. Batman had run out of ways to try to track her from the Batcave. He would prefer to locate her before her ultimatum expired at midnight.

It was time to hit the streets and gather what information he could in the criminal underworld.

Batman started in Crown Point, the most crime-ridden neighbourhood in the city, certain that one of the creeps there would have heard about Catwoman's whereabouts. But no matter which criminal he questioned, nobody had any useful information.

He came up empty in the mob den called the Cauldron. He found no trace of Catwoman in Crime Alley, either. She hadn't even set up a hideout in Toxic Acres, the poisoned suburb where criminals often laid low.

Somehow Catwoman had covered her tracks completely.

Bothered, Batman returned to the Batcave a few minutes before midnight. It frustrated him that Catwoman could hide so well in his city.

At midnight, Batman turned his attention to the TV. The mayor's emergency press conference was broadcast on all of the networks.

The mayor of Gotham strode out to the podium set up at City Hall in front of the media.

The mayor got right to the point. "We are sympathetic to Catwoman's concern for the legal status of cats in our city," he said. "But if she wants the law to change, she must work within the law and follow our legal process. We cannot and will not be swayed by criminal threats."

The press erupted with questions, but the mayor raised his hands for silence. "I will answer some questions," he said, "but first I have a recommendation for our citizens with cats. Put your pets in carriers for the night, so that Catwoman cannot steal them –"

The mayor was interrupted by a loud, jangling, rattling sound. It echoed at top volume out of every TV set, radio, MP3 player and computer speaker in the city. Cringing at the painful sound, the mayor tried to shout further instructions. The sistrum's rattle drowned him out.

In the Batcave, the cat Alfred had named Gladys sat up straight. Her ears perked up. She let out a loud yowl and leaped into motion, racing for the hidden exit.

Batman let her go. With the microchip in her collar, he could follow her with a GPS unit.

He set off after Gladys on the Batcycle, tracking her on a map on the cycle's computer screen.

The streets were full of cats, all rushing in the same direction. Batman had to swerve to avoid hitting some with his Batcycle. With the rivers of cats bounding towards the same single location, Batman didn't even need to track Gladys. He didn't understand how Catwoman was hoping to avoid capture – the torrent of converging cats would pinpoint her hideout precisely.

Batman followed the running parade of cats into the East End of Gotham City.

They passed a squad of police cars along the way that were heading in the same direction. The East End had been one of the worst areas of the city. However, recently it had been improving due to large-scale civic projects, like new parks and a new convention centre.

In fact, the cats were scurrying directly towards this new building.

The enormous building took up two city blocks, and had only been completed in the past month. It hadn't even been officially used yet, but was fully operational.

The front doors were wide open, and the cats were streaming inside.

Batman pulled to a stop in front of the convention centre.

He was amazed by the spectacle of thousands of cats scrambling to enter the building.

It was estimated that more than a million cats lived in Gotham, so if ten per cent answered Catwoman's summons with the sistrum, more than a hundred thousand cats were approaching the building or were already inside. And the percentage might be much higher.

The police cars stopped behind Batman's cycle. Commissioner Gordon hurried out to join Batman. "I've never seen anything like this," Gordon said. "Cats everywhere."

"Something for the history books," replied Batman.

Commissioner Gordon shook his head.

"How can we get in there?" Gordon asked. "She's surrounded by her own personal cat army. And we can't use tear gas or hurt the cats in any way. Catwoman was right about one thing – these cats are owned by the citizens of Gotham. Even if it was humane to attack innocent cats, we're talking about pet owners suing the city if any are harmed. I don't like this at all."

"I'll handle it," Batman growled.

He knew the layout of the new convention centre – Wayne Enterprises had been involved in the construction. Using his grapnel gun, Batman shot a wire up to the roof and then quickly scaled the side of the building. When he reached the top, he took firm hold of the wire and leaped off, swinging himself towards a huge wall of glass.

Boots first, Batman bashed through the pane, shards exploding all around him. He launched into the centre's main hall and landed on top of a snack bar kiosk. Batman retracted the grappling hook wire back into its launcher.

The wide, open room was packed with cats. As he had estimated, it wasn't merely thousands of cats – it was hundreds of thousands of cats.

They were every breed and size and colour and stripe. They were milling around the hall floor, getting into hissy spats, sleeping, playing, running back and forth, and just lazing around. The hall rang with cat noises: meows, yowls, chirps and purrs.

In the middle of it all, Catwoman perched on the sofa of a raised platform, looking radiant and pleased with herself.

"Welcome," Catwoman called. "You're too late to stop me, darling." She raised the jewelled sistrum. "I am sitting here with the glory of the goddess Bastet in my hand, surrounded by my friends. I am feeling quite powerful right now."

"The city will never cave in to your demands," Batman shouted. "You've done nothing but hurt your cause, and now you've cornered yourself, Catwoman."

"Really?" she shot back. "I have enough food for my sweeties for more than a month. Can the city hold out that long against a plague of rats?"

"I will stop this madness now," growled Batman.

"How?" Catwoman purred. "I have you surrounded."

Catwoman gave the sistrum a quick, sharp shake.

CLINK!

CLINK!

CLINK!

The rattle jangled across the convention centre. All the cats around Batman's snack kiosk began leaping up towards him. A cat can jump up to five times its own height, and the kiosk was only about two metres high. Which meant that some cats were grabbing onto the edges, and some were landing cleanly on the snack bar roof. They jumped up from all sides.

Batman could have kicked them off the roof, one by one, but as Commissioner Gordon had said, these cats were innocent victims. He couldn't hurt them.

In seconds, he was surrounded by hissing, arched cats threatening him with their claws.

As they began pouncing towards his boots, Batman raised his grapnel gun and shot the hook with its trailing wire up into the high rafters. He snagged a steel beam, and swung out over the ocean of snarling cats.

He had enough momentum to reach the sofa where Catwoman stood, but he never got there. As he arced near, she slung out her bullwhip and wrapped its tip around his ankle. With a surprisingly strong pull, she yanked him off the wire.

Batman tumbled into a horde of cats. They swarmed over him, screeching, howling, scratching, biting and whacking him with their paws.

One cat wouldn't have been a problem, nor ten cats. Batman could have brushed away a hundred cats. But he was overwhelmed by a thousand, ten thousand, a hundred thousand cats. They buried him deep under their hot furry bodies, crushing him with their combined weight.

Smashed flat by the cats, Batman tensed with the first fleeting feelings of panic. He would suffocate under the heap in moments.

Batman had no choice but to fight back.

He curled himself into a tight ball and then sprang his limbs outwards, knocking back cats in all directions.

Batman grabbed cats and hurled them from him. Their claws harmlessly scratched his Batsuit as he flung them away.

Using all his might, he managed to clear enough space to pull himself to his knees. He freed his head from the attacking cats.

Then he pulled a flare gun out of his Utility Belt, took aim and shot a blazing ball of light up into the rafters.

For a moment, nothing happened, and Batman worried that he'd missed his target.

HISSSSSSS!

A hissing noise filled the convention hall. He'd hit it – a fire detection heat sensor on the ceiling.

When burned by the hot flare, the sprinkler system soon activated.

Streams of water rained down from the ceiling all over the convention centre. The cats were stunned for a second, but then they reacted in absolute horror.

They were screaming and moaning as they scrambled around, desperately trying to escape the sudden shower.

Batman grinned as the cats scampered away. Water didn't hurt cats. They just didn't like getting wet – at all!

Catwoman shrieked in fury, as much from being dripping wet herself as having her plan foiled. She shook the sistrum and a few cats were brave enough to confront Batman. He jumped over them or sidestepped them easily. Most of the cats were fleeing through the exits or cowering along the drier sides of the hall.

"Hand over the sistrum," Batman insisted. "It doesn't belong to you."

In response, Catwoman snarled and snapped out her bullwhip. *CRAAAAACK!*

Batman dodged the whip's sting and rolled towards her, leaping up when he reached the base of the sofa. He tumbled into Catwoman, knocking her off her feet.

THUD!

Catwoman sprang up again and kicked at Batman's head. He stepped back and grabbed her foot, pulling her off balance. She scissor-kicked in the air and almost nailed him with her boot, but he ducked at the last second.

Landing on her feet, Catwoman flung herself into a back flip, hurtling towards Batman. He sidestepped and she tumbled off the sofa, dropping the sistrum.

CLACK CLACK CLACK!

It skittered across the wet floor, too far for her to reach it before Batman could.

With a scream of rage, Catwoman ran directly at Batman, who wasn't expecting her to charge. Instead of attacking him, she ran up his body and used his shoulders to launch herself into the air.

She grabbed onto his dangling grappling wire and swung across the convention hall. She headed for the broken window.

"Farewell, Bats!" Catwoman yelled back. "You beat me this time, but remember that a cat has nine lives – more than any bat!"

Then Catwoman dived through the window and disappeared into the night.

Batman stepped off the wet sofa and walked through the rainy convention hall towards the sistrum. He picked it up and put it into his Utility Belt.

Now that he knew what powers it held,

the hero realized that the instrument was no longer safe for public display.

He felt a startling soft sensation on his leg. He glanced down and was surprised to see a small tabby rubbing against his calf. Batman bent down and picked up the friendly cat.

"We're done here," he told Gladys. "Let's go home."

CATWOMAN

REAL NAME:
Selina Kyle

OCCUPATION:
Professional thief

BASE:
Gotham City

HEIGHT:
1 m 70 cm

WEIGHT:
57 kg

EYES:
Blue

HAIR:
Black

Like Bruce Wayne, Selina Kyle was orphaned at a young age. But unlike Bruce, Selina had no guardians or family fortune to support her. Growing up alone on the mean streets of Gotham, Selina was forced to resort to petty crime in order to survive. She soon became one of the city's most capable criminals. As Catwoman, Selina prowls the streets of Gotham, preying on the wealthy while guarding Gotham's fellow castaways.

- Selina's love of felines led her to choose a cat-related nickname. In fact, much of her stolen loot has been donated to cat-saving charities.

- The athletic Selina prefers to use her feline agility to evade her foes, but she won't hesitate to use her retractable claws.

- Catwoman may be a hardened criminal, but she also has a soft spot for Gotham's orphans. Proceeds from her high-profile crimes often go to Gotham City orphanages.

- Selina has been an ally to Batman several times. However, their alliances never last, as Selina is disinterested in ending her thieving ways.

BIOGRAPHIES

J. E. BRIGHT is the author of many novels, novelizations and novelty books for children and young adults. He lives in a sunny apartment in New York, USA with his difficult but soft cat, Mabel, and his sweet kitten, Bernard.

LUCIANO VECCHIO was born in 1982 and currently lives in Buenos Aires, Argentina. With experience in illustration, animation and comics, his works have been published in the US, Spain, UK, France and Argentina. His credits include *Ben 10* (DC Comics), *Cruel Thing* (Norma), *Unseen Tribe* (Zuda Comics) and *Sentinels* (Drumfish Productions).

GLOSSARY

alter ego if a person has an alter ego, then they have another identity that is often a secret. Bruce Wayne's alter ego is Batman.

ancient very old

artefact ancient object made by human beings, such as a tool or weapon

feline cat, or like a cat

patron someone who gives money to help another person, activity or cause

prowler someone or something that sneaks around quietly as if hunting for prey

sistrum ancient Egyptian musical instrument

socialites wealthy or important people

swarm group of animals that gathers or moves in large numbers

tuxedo man's suit worn for formal occasions. It usually includes a black jacket and smart trousers, a white shirt and a bow tie.

DISCUSSION QUESTIONS

1. Bruce doesn't like the appetizers he eats at the party. What are your least favourite foods?

2. Batman and Alfred adopt a cat as a pet. Do you have any pets? What kind of animal would be your dream pet? Talk about pets and their place in your life.

3. This book has ten illustrations. Which one is your favourite? Why?

WRITING PROMPTS

1. Bruce Wayne knows that Selina Kyle is also Catwoman, but Selina doesn't know that Bruce is also Batman. What kinds of advantages does this give Bruce? Write down as many as you can.

2. Selina used the symbol of a cat for her costume. Bruce used a bat for his. If you were a super hero, which animal would you choose as your symbol? Write about your costume, then draw it.

3. Imagine you're an archaeologist who digs up an ancient Egyptian artefact. What does the artefact look like? What was it used for? Does it have any special powers? Write about your artefact, then draw it.